This **Orchard** book belongs to

_____

Mouse

Zebra

Giraffe

Crocodile

Mole

Koala　　　Camel　　　Lion　　　Dog　　　Hippo

To Hildegard and Vincent

ORCHARD BOOKS
338 Euston Road, London NW1 3BH
Orchard Books Australia
Level 17/207 Kent Street, Sydney, NSW 2000

First published in 2011 by Orchard Books
First published in paperback in 2013

ISBN 978 1 40831 441 8

Illustrations © Britta Teckentrup 2011

A CIP catalogue record for this book is available from the British Library.

1 3 5 7 9 10 8 6 4 2

Printed in China

Orchard Books is a division of Hachette Children's Books,
an Hachette UK company.

www.hachette.co.uk

The Wheels on the Bus

Britta Teckentrup

The wheels on the bus go round and round,
Round and round, round and round,
The wheels on the bus go round and round,
All day long.

The wipers on the bus go swish swish swish,
Swish swish swish, swish swish swish,
The wipers on the bus go swish swish swish,
All day long.

The people on the bus go up and down,
Up and down, up and down,
The people on the bus go up and down,
All day long.

The babies on the bus go, "Wah wah wah,
Wah wah wah, wah wah wah,"
The babies on the bus go, "Wah wah wah,"
All day long.

The parents on the bus go, "Shh shh shh,
Shh shh shh, shh shh shh,"
The parents on the bus go, "Shh shh shh,"
All day long.

The mamas on the bus go, "I love you,
I love you, I love you,"
The papas on the bus go, "I love you, too,"
All day long.

The wheels on the bus go round and round,
Round and round, round and round,
The wheels on the bus go round and round,
All day long.